PowerKids Readers:

# The Bilingual Library of the United States of America™

Bilingual Edition
English/Spanish
Edición bilingüe

# SOUTH DAKOTA
# DAKOTA DEL SUR

**VANESSA BROWN**

TRADUCCIÓN AL ESPAÑOL: MARÍA CRISTINA BRUSCA

The Rosen Publishing Group's
PowerKids Press™ & **Editorial Buenas Letras**™
New York

Published in 2006 by The Rosen Publishing Group, Inc.
29 East 21st Street, New York, NY 10010

First Edition

Book Design: Albert B. Hanner
Photo Credits:  Cover, p. 21, 30 (State Nickname) © Joseph Sohm; Visions of America/Corbis; p. 5 Albert B. Hanner; pp. 7, 31 (border) © 2002, Geoaltas; p. 9 © Charles E. Rotkin/Corbis p. 11 © Ron Sanford/Corbis; p.p. 13, 30 (state Motto), 31 (prarie) © Robert vander Hilst/Corbis; p.p. 15, 31 (Sitting Bull), (Red Cloud) © Corbis; p.p. 17, 31 (Wilder), (Humphrey), (Anderson) © Bettmann/Corbis; p.p. 19, 31 (cattle) © Tom Bean/Corbis; p. 23 © Nik Wheeler/Corbis; p.p. 25, 30 (capital) © Donald C. Johnson/Corbis; p.p. 25; p. 30 (State flower) © Markus Botzek/zefa/Corbis, (State tree) © Tom Bean/Corbis, (State Animal) © W. Perry Conway/Corbis; p. 31 (Brokaw) © Owen Franken/Corbis.

Library of Congress Cataloging-in-Publication Data

Brown, Vanessa, 1963–
  South Dakota / Vanessa Brown ; traducción al español, María Cristina Brusca. —1st ed.
    p. cm. — (The bilingual library of the United States of America)
  Includes index.
  ISBN 1-4042-3107-2 (library binding)
  1. South Dakota–Juvenile literature. I. Title. II. Series.
  F651.3.B76 2006
  978.3–dc22
                                                2005026287

Manufactured in the United States of America

Due to the changing nature of Internet links, Editorial Buenas Letras has developed an online list of Web sites related to the subject of this book. This site is updated regularly. Please use this link to access the list:

http://www.buenasletraslinks.com/ls/southdakota

# Contents

# Contenido

## Welcome to South Dakota

These are the flag and seal of the state of South Dakota. The seal has a banner with the state motto on it. It reads, "Under God the People Rule."

---

## Bienvenidos a Dakota del Sur

Estos son la bandera y el escudo del estado de Dakota del Sur. En el escudo hay una banda con el lema del estado. El lema dice, "El pueblo gobierna bajo la gracia de Dios".

## South Dakota Flag and State Seal

Bandera y escudo del estado de Dakota del Sur

## South Dakota Geography

South Dakota is in the American Midwest. South Dakota borders the states of Wyoming, Montana, North Dakota, Minnesota, Iowa, and Nebraska.

---

## Geografía de Dakota del Sur

Dakota del Sur está en la región central de los Estados Unidos, conocida como el *Midwest*. Dakota del Sur linda con los estados de Wyoming, Montana, Dakota del Norte, Minnesota, Iowa y Nebraska.

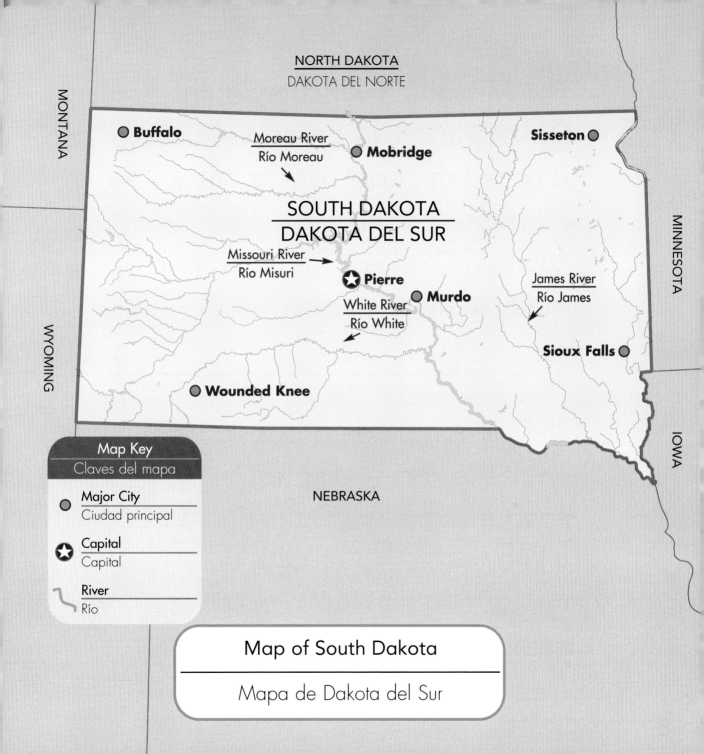

NORTH DAKOTA
DAKOTA DEL NORTE

MONTANA

Buffalo

Moreau River
Río Moreau

Mobridge

Sisseton

SOUTH DAKOTA
DAKOTA DEL SUR

MINNESOTA

Missouri River
Río Misuri

Pierre

James River
Río James

WYOMING

White River
Río White

Murdo

Sioux Falls

Wounded Knee

IOWA

## Map Key
### Claves del mapa

Major City
Ciudad principal

Capital
Capital

River
Río

NEBRASKA

## Map of South Dakota

### Mapa de Dakota del Sur

The Missouri River cuts South Dakota into two areas. One area is called the east river country. The other area is the west river country. The best farmland is in the east river country.

---

El río Misuri divide a Dakota del Sur en dos regiones. Una región se conoce como la zona al este del río y la otra como la zona al oeste del río. Las mejores tierras de cultivo están en la zona este.

## Wheat Fields near Sturgis, South Dakota

Cultivos de trigo cerca de Sturgis, Dakota del Sur

The Black Hills National Forest is on the southwestern border of South Dakota. It has pine forests, caves, lakes, and prairies. Bison, elk, and coyotes live in the Black Hills.

---

El Bosque Nacional Black Hills está en la frontera suroeste de Dakota del Sur. Tiene bosques de pinos, grutas, lagos y praderas. En Black Hills viven bisontes, alces y coyotes.

Bison in the Black Hills National Forest

Bisontes en el Bosque Nacional Black Hills

## South Dakota History

Since the 1700s, South Dakota has been home to the Dakota, Lakota, and Nakota peoples. In the Lakota language, the word *Dakota* means "friends."

---

## Historia de Dakota del Sur

Desde los años 1700, Dakota del Sur ha sido el hogar de los grupos nativos Dakota, Lakota y Nakota. En el idioma lakota, la palabra *dakota* quiere decir "amigos".

## Lakota Sioux

Lakota-Sioux

Sitting Bull was a Lakota chief. He was born in what would become Grand River, South Dakota. Sitting Bull led his people to fight against the U.S. government, which was taking their land.

---

Toro Sentado fue un jefe Lakota. Nació en Dakota del Sur, en lo que ahora conocemos como Grand River. Toro Sentado dirigió la lucha de los lakotas contra el gobierno de los E.U.A., que estaba tomando sus tierras.

Sitting Bull (1831–1890)

Toro Sentado (1831–1890)

Laura Ingalls Wilder is the writer of the Little House books. These books talk about her days in Kansas and Dakota territories. She lived from 1867 to 1957.

---

Laura Ingalls Wilder es la autora de la serie de libros "La casa de la pradera". En estos libros, Ingalls describe su infancia en los territorios de Kansas y Dakota. Laura Ingalls Wilder vivió de 1867 a 1957.

Laura Ingalls Wilder

## Living in South Dakota

Half of South Dakotans live in towns or cities. The other half live in rural areas, such as farms in the countryside. Most of the state's land is used for farming or raising cattle.

---

## La vida en Dakota del Sur

La mitad de los surdakoteños vive en pueblos y ciudades. La otra mitad vive en zonas rurales, en ranchos y granjas. La mayoría de la tierra del estado está dedicada a la agricultura y a la cría de ganado.

Cowboys Working in South Dakota

Vaqueros trabajando en Dakota del Sur

Many people visit Mount Rushmore. A sculpture on Mount Rushmore shows four important U.S. presidents. They are George Washington, Thomas Jefferson, Theodore Roosevelt, and Abraham Lincoln.

---

Mucha gente visita el Monte Rushmore. Una escultura en el Monte Rushmore representa a cuatro importantes presidentes de los E.U.A. Estos son George Washington, Thomas Jefferson, Theodore Roosevelt y Abraham Lincoln.

Mount Rushmore National Memorial

Monumento Nacional Monte Rushmore

## South Dakota Today

A new memorial monument is being built near Mount Rushmore. It honors the Oglala Sioux chief Crazy Horse. When it is finished, it will be the largest sculpture in the world!

---

## Dakota del Sur, hoy

Cerca del Monte Rushmore se está construyendo un nuevo monumento en memoria de *Crazy Horse* (Caballo Loco) un jefe de la tribu Oglala-Sioux. ¡Cuando se termine será la escultura más grande del mundo!

Crazy Horse Memorial

Monumento a Caballo Loco

Sioux Falls, Rapid City, Aberdeen, and Pierre are important cities in South Dakota. Pierre is the capital of the state.

---

Sioux Falls, Rapid City, Aberdeen y Pierre son ciudades importantes de Dakota del Sur. Pierre es la capital del estado.

State Capitol in Pierre, South Dakota

Capitolio del estado en Pierre, Dakota del Sur

# Activity:
## Let´s draw South Dakota's State Flower

The pasque flower became South Dakota's state flower in 1903.

# Actividad:
## Dibujemos la flor del estado de Dakota del Sur

La anémona pulsatilla es la flor del estado de Dakota del Sur.

**1**

Draw a small circle for the center of the flower. Draw six ovals that touch the circle.

Dibuja un círculo pequeño como centro de la flor. Dibuja seis óvalos que toquen ese círculo.

**2**

Use the ovals as guides to draw the tips of the petals.

Usa los óvalos como guías para dibujar las puntas de los pétalos.

**3**

Erase the extra lines. Your drawing should look like this.

Borra las líneas que sobren. Tu dibujo tendría que verse como éste.

**4**

Draw tiny circles in the center of the flower.

Dibuja círculos muy pequeñitos adentro del centro de la flor.

**5**

Add lines inside the petals. Draw the leaves around the flower. Finish your drawing with shading.

Agrega líneas adentro de los pétalos. Dibuja las hojas alrededor de la flor. Sombrea tu dibujo para terminarlo.

# Timeline

| | Cronología |
|---|---|

Lakota, Dakota, and Nakota peoples arrive from central Canada, Minnesota and Wisconsin.

**1700s** Grupos Lakota, Dakota y Nakota llegan desde Minnesota, Wisconsin y el centro de Canadá.

The La Verendrye brothers are the first Europeans to reach South Dakota.

**1743** Los hermanos La Verendrye son los primeros europeos en llegar a Dakota del Sur.

The United States buys the Louisiana Territory, which includes South Dakota, from France.

**1803** Los Estados Unidos le compran a Francia el Territorio de Luisiana, que incluye Dakota del Sur.

South Dakota becomes the fortieth state in the Union.

**1889** Dakota del Sur se convierte en el estado cuarenta de la Unión.

Gutzon Borglum begins Mount Rushmore National Memorial.

**1927** Gutzon Borglum comienza el Monumento Nacional en Monte Rushmore.

South Dakota becomes the leader in gold production in the United States.

**1944** El estado de Dakota del Sur llega a ser el mayor productor de oro de E.U.A

Carole Hillard becomes the first woman in South Dakota to be elected lieutenant governor.

**1995** Carole Hillard es la primera mujer electa como vicegobernadora del estado.

# South Dakota Events

## Eventos en Dakota del Sur

| South Dakota Events | Eventos en Dakota del Sur |
|---|---|
| **February**<br>SDSU Annual Wacipi in Brookings | Febrero<br>Wacipi anual SDSU, en Brookings |
| **March**<br>Black Hills Horse Expo in Rapid City | Marzo<br>Exposición equina de las Lomas Negras, en Rapid City |
| **May**<br>Korczak Day in South Dakota | Mayo<br>Día Korczak en Dakota del Sur, |
| **June**<br>Crazy Horse Volksmarch in Crazy Horse<br>Wild Bill Hickok Days in Deadwood | Junio<br>Crazy Horse Volksmarch, en Crazy Horse<br>Días de Wild Bill Hickok, en Deadwood |
| **July**<br>Sioux Falls Jazz and Blues Festival | Julio<br>Festival de jazz y blues, en Sioux Falls |
| **September**<br>South Dakota Festival of Books in Deadwood and Sioux Falls | Septiembre<br>Festival del libro de Dakota del Sur, en Deadwood y Sioux Falls |
| **October**<br>Black Hills Pow Wow (He Sapa Wacipi) in Rapid City<br>Mount Rushmore Marathon in Rapid City<br>Dakota Days at the University of South Dakota in Vermillion | Octubre<br>Pow Wow de la Lomas Negras (He Sapa Wacipi), en Rapid City<br>Maratón del Monte Rushmore, en Rapid City<br>Días Dakota, en la Universidad de Dakota del Sur, en Vermillion |
| **December**<br>First Night Sioux Falls, in Sioux Falls | Diciembre<br>Primera noche en Sioux Falls |

# South Dakota Facts/
## Datos sobre Dakota del Sur

Population
754,844

Población
754,844

Capital
Pierre

Capital
Pierre

State Motto
Under God
the People Rule

Lema del estado
El pueblo gobierna bajo
la gracia de Dios

State Flower
Pasque flower

Flor del estado
Anémona pulsatilla

State Bird
Ring-necked pheasant

Ave del estado
Faisán de golilla blanca

State Nickname
The Mount
Rushmore State

Mote del estado
El Estado del Monte
Rushmore

State Tree
Black Hill spruce

Árbol del estado
Pino Black Hill

State Animal
Coyote

Animal del estado
Coyote

# Famous South Dakotans/
## Surdakoteños famosos

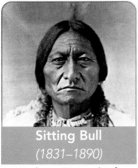

**Sitting Bull**
*(1831–1890)*

Dakota Sioux chief
Jefe Dakota-Sioux

**Red Cloud**
*(1822–1909)*

Oglala Sioux chief
Jefe Oglala-Sioux

**Laura Ingalls Wilder**
*(1867–1957)*

Author
Escritora

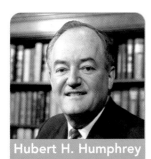

**Hubert H. Humphrey**
*(1911–1978)*

U.S. vice president
Vicepresidente de E.U.A.

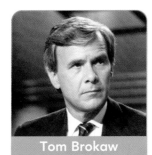

**Tom Brokaw**
*(1940–   )*

News commentator
Comentarista de noticias

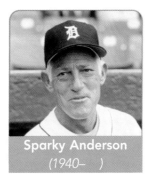

**Sparky Anderson**
*(1940–   )*

Baseball manager
Entrenador de béisbol

# Words to Know/Palabras que debes saber

**banner**
banda

**border**
frontera

**cattle**
ganado

**prairie**
pradera

**Here are more books to read about South Dakota:**
Otros libros que puedes leer sobre Dakota del Sur:

**In English/En inglés:**

*South Dakota Facts and Symbols*
by Feeney, Kathy
Bridgestone Books, 2003

*South Dakota*
by Heinrichs, Ann
Compass Point Books, 2003

Words in English: 312          Palabras en español: 358

# Index

# Índice